The Palace of Versailles, France, 1783.

A crowd has gathered to witness the launch of the first hot air balloon . . .

. . . with living pilots.

Queen Marie Antoinette and King Louis XVI were in attendance, of course . . .

. . . as were many distinguished guests, including the American diplomat Benjamin Franklin.

The balloon launched successfully and flew for two miles at an altitude of fifteen hundred feet before landing safely in a field.

Very impressive. But what use is a balloon?

You might ask, "What is the use of a baby?"

Babies. Balloons. All is potential.

The Sheep, the Rooster, and the Duck

By MATT PHELAN

Greenwillow Books

An Imprint of HarperCollins*Publishers*

Chapter One

Two years later

A carriage drawn by a single horse sped down a forest road. The driver, Edward Bancroft, snapped his whip and yelled, "Yah!" as he raced deeper into the woods. The darkness enveloped him.

Suddenly Bancroft pulled hard on the reins. The horse reared and kicked, snorted and whinnied.

Four men on horseback, pistols drawn, blocked the road before him.

"Highwaymen!" exclaimed Bancroft. "I carry no money with me. The carriage is empty. See for yourself."

The highwaymen parted, allowing a fifth rider to join the blockade. He was a large man in a black cloak, his face hidden by a strange, birdlike mask.

"Edward Bancroft?" said the man in the mask.

"Yes, I am Bancroft."

"Edward Bancroft, secretary to ambassador Benjamin Franklin?"

"Yes," said Bancroft.

"Edward Bancroft . . . the English spy?"

Bancroft said nothing.

"You will give me that letter you carry, Monsieur Bancroft. Or else," said the masked man.

Two highwaymen took aim.

Bancroft reached into his cloak and slowly removed an envelope.

"Wise choice, Monsieur Bancroft. I thank you for keeping this exchange pleasant. Return to Monsieur Franklin's house and continue to gather information. But from this night forward, you are not spying for England. You work for me."

The masked man approached. He reached for the letter.

What can only be described as a fast-moving shadow soared between them, snatching the letter from a startled Bancroft.

"*Bête Noire!*" screamed a highwayman.

"Get that letter!" bellowed the masked man.

Pistols fired. But the shadow was small and agile. It flipped and zipped across the road.

A highwayman drew his sword. With a flash of steel, the shadow knocked the weapon from his hand.

When the dust from the road settled, the shadow had vanished. With the letter.

"*Bête Noire,*" muttered the masked man. "We shall meet again. Very soon."

❧ Chapter Two ❧

At midnight the village was completely still, not a sound to be heard nor movement to be seen.

Except for a small shadow. It slipped swiftly from the wall to the well to the side of the barn. The moon emerged from behind a cloud, revealing the shadow was a rooster. The rooster wore a black satin mask and kept a sword in a sash at its waist. He held the letter.

The rooster hopped through the barn window and landed silently on the dirt-and-straw-covered floor.

The rooster glanced around. The coast was clear. He drew his sword and pressed the point against a knot of wood on the barn wall.

A trapdoor in the floor cranked open, and soft light spilled up into the barn. The rooster slipped down the hatch, which closed behind him.

"About time," said the duck.

"An artist cannot be rushed, my dear Jean-Luc," said the rooster.

"Was it him, Pierre?" A sheep turned from studying a large map on the wall. The map showed various notes, lines, and circles. "Was it Cagliostro?" asked the sheep.

"Most certainly, Bernadette," said the rooster. "He is still wearing that ridiculous mask. As if *he* could have a beak."

"Pierre, be a fine fellow and read the letter," said the duck, Jean-Luc.

Pierre, the rooster, broke the wax seal with a flourish.

He cleared his throat and began to read:

My dearest darling honey loaf,

The days are simply unbearable without the sweet nectar of your laugh, the rich wine of your eyes, and the fine cheese of your company! How dost I miss thee? Let me now carefully count the ways . . .

Pierre looked up. "There are a lot of ways. Should I go on?"

"Yes," said Jean-Luc, hopping from his stool to grab a candle. He brought it close to the back of the letter. "But *now*, please."

The candlelight illuminated more writing, hidden between the lines of the love letter.

"Oh ho! Invisible ink. Most clever!" said Pierre. "Yes, here we are. It seems that Benjamin Franklin is developing some new plans for hot air balloons. And they are not pleasant."

Bernadette, the sheep, slammed her hoof on the worktable. "Humans," she muttered.

The sheep turned and examined her wall. Besides the map, it was covered with diagrams: beautiful watercolor designs for balloons of all sizes and shapes, navigational aids, new methods of propulsion, ingenious baskets

with clever storage compartments, and more.

"Such a lovely thing, the lighter-than-air balloon. Why can it not remain so?" she asked.

"Sadly, it is not the way of human beings to leave well enough alone," said Jean-Luc. The duck took the letter, read it silently, then set it alight with the candle. "That is why we will stop them."

"With style and finesse," added Pierre, swishing his sword through the air and extinguishing the flame.

A look of steely determination grew in Bernadette's eyes.

"Step one: we need our *own* spy in the house of Benjamin Franklin."

⟶ Chapter Three ⟵

Benjamin Franklin, inventor, diplomat, and many other things, sat at his desk in his sun-dappled study. Years ago he had been sent to France to seek assistance for the American colonies in their struggle against England. In France, hating England was a national pastime, so Franklin's mission was a great success. Now the War of Independence was over, the Treaty of Paris signed. Benjamin Franklin's time in France was drawing to a close. There were fewer meetings at court these days, fewer salons to attend, and fewer visitors to entertain.

Benjamin Franklin's great mind was free to wander.

The details of the household operated without his attention, thanks to the skill and dedication of the château's caretaker and sole servant. Although only ten years of age, Emile excelled at his job. Orphaned after the death of his father, the previous caretaker, Emile found great purpose and satisfaction in his duties, and he devoted his life to his work.

At this moment, Emile was placing the freshly polished silver candlestick holders in their places. He examined them. He moved one a fraction of an inch to the left. Another, a bit to the right.

Satisfied at last, Emile retrieved his broom from the cupboard (right side, in front of the neatly stacked buckets and the ironed and folded rags).

Emile carried the broom up the stairs and gently

knocked on the study door.

"Monsieur Franklin?"

"Come in, Emile."

Emile slipped in without
a sound, a skill he had
perfected.

"Ah yes!" said Franklin.
"Sweeping time is upon
us again. I know I said I
would be away from my desk
at this hour, but I had a few more ideas to get down on
paper."

"I can come back."

"No, I know how you enjoy your schedule, my boy.
Please go ahead while I finish here."

"Yes, Monsieur." Emile began to sweep, starting in the
northwest corner as usual.

Franklin continued his work, carefully sketching in his private journal. He glanced over at Emile.

"Emile, I require your expertise."

"Something dusted, Monsieur Franklin?"

"No."

"Your desk polished?"

"No."

"Laundry?"

"No. Your *expertise*, Emile. I have noticed your sketches about the house. Drawings of the stables and animals."

"I am sorry if they were left in view. I shall—"

"You are missing the point." Franklin chuckled. "They are quite good drawings. Now, *this*"—he lifted up his journal—"this is somewhat off. You have talent and an eye. Pray tell, where have I gone wrong?"

Emile examined the drawing of a hot air balloon.

"The bottom of the balloon should taper more. You have made it too round."

"Ah! So I have. It is as round as my own belly. I do love France, but the delicious cuisine is expanding my circumference to an alarming degree. Thank you for your astute observation. Do you like balloons?"

"I have heard of them, but I have not yet seen one."

"Oh, they are splendid! Such potential."

Franklin paused. He turned the page of his journal and showed Emile another sketch: a fleet of hot air balloons gliding over a battlefield. Notes about air currents and lightweight weaponry filled the margins.

"I am ashamed to say that my mind could not leave it a simple wonder. I had to imagine more destructive uses. A habit developed from years of revolution."

He turned the page. Emile caught a glimpse of another design with the words *Heat Ray* written above

it. Franklin closed the notebook.

"What is your ambition, Emile?"

"Monsieur?"

"What do you want to do with your life?"

"Well . . . I would like to improve on my housekeeping skills. Perhaps branch out into basic repair work."

"Is that all?"

Emile thought.

"Maybe one day I'd work in a large mansion, with a staff. But I am extremely happy here, Monsieur!"

"Would you run the staff or—"

"Oh no. I would just be a member of the staff," said Emile.

"Hmm." Franklin studied Emile for a moment.

"Help yourself to as much paper as you need for your drawings, Emile."

"Thank you, Monsieur. You are very kind."

Franklin rose and walked to the door of the study.

"Monsieur Franklin, your notebook. Shouldn't you lock it in your desk drawer?"

Franklin sighed. "I suppose so. Some places have a problem with mice; France seems to have a problem with *spies*."

He locked the notebook in the right-side drawer and closed the desktop.

A sharp knock sounded at the study door.

"Bancroft! My dedicated secretary. What *perfect* timing," said Franklin, opening the door.

"Mr. Franklin, your presence is required at the Palace of Versailles."

⤙ Chapter Four ⤚

$\mathcal{E}$mile was on his way to prepare the carriage when the bell for the servants' entrance clanged. Without waiting for Emile to open the door fully, a girl about his age shoved her way into the kitchen.

"Delivery for Monsieur Franklin!" she announced.

"Wha— wait! You can't just barge in here!" sputtered Emile.

The girl placed a wooden box on the counter. "How else can I deliver this?" she demanded.

"You can hand it to *me*. I am in charge here."

"Pfft," said the girl.

"Excuse me?"

"This box contains a soufflé. A *soufflé*. Can you be trusted with a soufflé?"

"Um."

"This soufflé is a gift from Madame Deneuve."

"Oh. Monsieur Franklin is quite fond of Madame Deneuve."

"You could say that." The girl glared intensely. "Do you trust yourself to care for the soufflé without flattening it?"

"Well . . . "

"Exactly. Allow me to do my work."

"Yes. I'll . . . um . . . just be in the stable, preparing the carriage," said Emile, backing out of the kitchen.

"You do that. I will let myself out."

"Good. Shut the door tight when you do," Emile said from the threshold. "Please," he added quickly.

"Pfft," said the girl.

Once Emile was gone, she opened the box, carefully removed the soufflé, and placed it by the open window. Then she returned her attention to the box. She ran a finger along the edge and pressed.

A small door slid open on the side of the box. A mouse

crept out. The girl gave the mouse a thumbs-up. The mouse returned the gesture, then dashed off the counter, across the kitchen, through the door, and up the stairs.

Emile walked to the stable, mentally compiling a list of everything Monsieur Franklin might need for his trip to Versailles. He was startled to see that Monsieur Bancroft had already prepared the horse and carriage. Franklin was opening the carriage door, humming to himself.

"I am sorry, Monsieur. There was a delivery—"

Not to worry, Emile," said Franklin. "We Americans are self-reliant in many ways."

Bancroft coughed and tightened the bridle on the horse.

"While you are away, shall I scrub the floors or perhaps whitewash the fence by the barn?" asked Emile. "Or I could attend to the squeaking floorboard or—"

Franklin climbed into the carriage and turned to Emile.

"Emile, my dear boy. I have complete faith in you. Use your own *initiative*. If you see something that needs attention, attend to it. Do not wait for permission."

"Yes, Monsieur Franklin. Thank you."

"Bancroft," said Franklin, tapping the ceiling of the carriage with his cane. "Let us be off. I am sure you are equally curious about this summons from the king!"

Bancroft gritted his teeth and snapped the reins. The carriage set off down the road.

Emile returned to the house. He took a deep breath. A full day to himself. The house would be immaculate when Monsieur Franklin returned.

He peered cautiously into the kitchen. The intimidating girl had left. Fortune was indeed smiling upon Emile.

After some consideration, he began in Monsieur Franklin's study. This was an excellent time to dust the books and carefully inspect the alphabetical order. When Monsieur Franklin was excited, he occasionally placed books quite haphazardly.

Emile froze in the doorway.

A mouse sat on Monsieur Franklin's desk!

Not only that, but the mouse had apparently unlocked the desk drawer, removed the journal, and—Emile blinked several times—was now copying information from the journal into a tiny notebook with a teensy pencil.

Some places have a problem with mice, Monsieur Franklin had said. *France seems to have a problem with spies.*

A mouse spy?

"Stop!" shouted Emile. It was the only thing he could think to say.

The mouse snapped the tiny notebook shut and leaped from the desk, zipping between Emile's legs and out the door.

Emile darted to the desk. The journal lay open to a page of Franklin's balloon designs. As he closed it, a few more pages turned. Emile stared down at the Heat Ray. Had the mouse seen this design?

He placed the journal back in the drawer. It would have to remain unlocked. How could he explain this? He must catch that mouse, or he would never be believed.

Emile tore out of the study and down the stairs. No mouse. At a noise from the kitchen, he ran there.

Nothing was amiss. The door was closed. The soufflé sat on the counter.

Slowly, silently, the soufflé began to expand. It grew larger, rounder, fuller—and then it lifted from the counter. Suspended beneath the inflated soufflé was a basket, and in the basket was the mouse.

It waved a tiny paw at Emile.

And then the soufflé, basket, and mouse spy drifted out the window and up into the air.

Chapter Five

Fifi was not the fastest horse, but she was Emile's own horse. Emile galloped as swiftly as Fifi could manage, following the soufflé balloon and the mouse spy across the countryside.

The balloon did not fly terribly high, but it was fast. Surprisingly, it seemed able to move with definite direction. But Emile was gaining on it.

He thought briefly of his cleaning schedule back at the house. This excursion would play havoc with his dusting regimen, but it must be done. The secrets in Monsieur Franklin's notebook must not be stolen by anyone, including rodents.

Emile had ridden with his eyes only on the balloon. He realized now that he had no idea where he was. Looking ahead, he spotted a distinctive building through the trees.

The Palace of Versailles.

The balloon shifted course slightly and flew east of the palace. Emile followed. The trees parted to reveal a small village and an enormous barn. Strange, he thought, as

the balloon glided toward the barn. Emile halted Fifi and watched.

A hatch opened in the barn's roof and the delivery girl climbed out. She pulled up a very long pole. At the end of the pole was a net. She held the pole high and the soufflé balloon drifted right into the net. Then the pole, the girl, and the mouse spy all disappeared back down the hatch.

Now what? thought Emile.

He had not considered what he would do when he caught the mouse. And now it seemed he would also need to speak with that girl again, a prospect that made him distinctly uneasy.

But Monsieur Franklin himself was visiting the palace. If need be, Emile could enlist his help. Of course, that would be a last resort. This mouse spy business was largely his own fault, and he must take care of it. That was what a professional caretaker did.

Emile urged Fifi down the road. The village was exceptionally ordinary. *Perfectly* ordinary, you might say. Each building was more quaint than any Emile had ever

seen. The well in the square was in immaculate repair. The gravel and dirt road was smooth and even, as though he and Fifi were the first to trod upon it. In fact, Emile could not detect a single inhabitant. No one in the shops. No one bustling to or fro. Complete stillness and silence. He dismounted and tied Fifi to a post by a pristine water trough. Fifi drank contentedly, and Emile crept toward the barn.

The bottom half of the door was closed, but the top half was wide open. Cautiously, he looked inside. It held bales of hay, farm equipment, buckets—the usual things found in a barn.

Emile gently lifted the latch and stepped inside. Above him was a loft. Also deserted. Where could the girl and mouse have gone? It was imposs—

Emile froze. He stared at the loft. He examined the walls of the barn. One benefit of drawing is that it develops the ability to see, to focus on details and establish correct proportions.

This barn did not have correct proportions. The interior was much smaller than the exterior. There was more to this barn than met the eye. Literally.

Emile took a few steps toward the wall. There were two prominent knots in a post. Not unusual in barn wood, perhaps, but these two knots were slightly recessed into the post. Emile chose a knot and pushed.

It was not the correct knot.

One knot, as we have seen, opened the hidden ramp that led down to the secret headquarters. This second knot, which Emile pushed, opened a trapdoor directly beneath his feet. Emile dropped down a chute in complete darkness until he landed on some hay in a cage, in a room glowing with lamplight.

The girl stared at him in surprise. Behind the girl

emerged a sheep, a rooster, and a duck. The mouse sat on a large workbench eating some cheese. It pointed at Emile and squeaked accusingly.

"Manners, Felix, please," said the sheep.

"I am impressed, frankly," said the duck. "He pushed the wrong button, but he did *find* the secret buttons. Bravo, boy!"

"Thank you . . . ?" said Emile. The sheep and duck had just spoken. Words. He was amazed, but they were also being polite and complimentary. He agreed with the sheep. Manners were important.

"I am sorry to disturb you, but I believe that mouse *spied* on Monsieur Franklin."

"Of course he did! Felix is the best spy in France," said the girl. "You were in the wrong place at the wrong time. I say we make this boy disappear. Pierre, your sword!"

"Sophie! Please calm down," said the sheep. "I am sure that will not be necessary."

The rooster, however, had indeed drawn his rapier. He stepped closer to the cage. He wore a black satin mask. Emile inched back.

"Ha-HA!" laughed the rooster. He jabbed the lock of the cage with his sword and released Emile. "I like him!"

Emile climbed out of the cage and looked around. The room was full of maps, swords, strange clock-like devices, and a laboratory of vials containing mysterious liquids. The most exquisite balloon designs he had ever seen were tacked to the walls.

"Since the cat, as they say, appears to be out of the bag, allow us to introduce ourselves," said the sheep. "My name is Bernadette."

"Jean-Luc," said the duck. "A pleasure to meet you."

"And I am Pierre," said the rooster, tucking his sword

in his sash. "Perhaps you have heard of me by my other name: Bête Noire, the Scourge of the Underworld!"

"I am afraid not, Pierre," said Emile. "I do not get out much. And I never mingle with the underworld," he added hastily.

"And I believe you have met Sophie," said Bernadette. "She is an invaluable friend and team member."

"Team?" asked Emile.

"Wherever there is injustice . . . " said Sophie.

" . . . Nefarious plots . . . " said the sheep.

" . . . Threats to society . . . " said the rooster.

"We are there to thwart them," finished the duck.

"We also design lighter-than-air balloons," said the sheep with a hint of pride.

"Wait a minute," said Emile excitedly. "Are you *the* sheep, rooster, and duck from the famous Montgolfier balloon flight? The first living creatures to ascend in a balloon?"

"The very same," said Pierre. "You didn't think they would trust that task to an *ordinary* group of animals?"

"I had, actually," said Emile.

"All part of the plan," said Jean-Luc.

"Please forgive me," stammered Emile. "My name is Emile. I am the caretaker of Monsieur Franklin's chateau in Passy, and his general servant."

"We *know*," huffed Sophie.

"But if you sent a spy to Passy," said Emile, "that means Monsieur Franklin's plans are—"

"A threat to society, yes. But not quite yet," said Jean-Luc.

"He did not mean his designs to be a threat," said Emile. "Monsieur Franklin is a genius inventor. He can't help it."

"It is not Franklin we are concerned about," said Pierre. "There are other actors in our little play. Villains of a high order."

A sudden clanging of cowbells sounded through the secret headquarters.

"Visitors," said Bernadette.

"Villains?" asked Emile.

"Worse," said Sophie. "That insipid queen."

∽ Chapter Six ∽

Sophie led Emile from the barn to the well in the square of the quiet village.

"Where are the villagers?" asked Emile.

"Villagers? It's just my father taking care of the buildings, and me working with Bernadette," said Sophie.

Bernadette, Pierre, and Jean-Luc ambled into a pen beside the barn. Pierre was not wearing his mask. They were behaving like ordinary farm animals.

"I don't understand," Emile said, taking the water bucket Sophie handed him.

"This is not a real village," said Sophie. "This is Trianon. A plaything for *her*."

Emile followed Sophie's glare. Skipping down the path was Marie Antoinette, Queen of France. Emile gasped. Known throughout the world for her extravagant tastes, flamboyant fashion sense, and elaborate wigs, today she

wore a plain—yet perfectly clean and tailored—frock. Her real hair (*wigless!*) was tied in a simple braid.

Sophie attached a hook to the bucket and began to lower it into the well.

"She finds it amusing to 'play peasant.' We are the decoration."

"That . . . that is very strange," said Emile.

"Welcome to Versailles," said Sophie.

"Tra la la," sang Marie Antoinette, entering the square. "A fine ordinary day in quaint Trianon! We are poor, but very happy here!"

"Pfft," muttered Sophie.

"Oh!" said the queen as she approached the well. "If it isn't dear, simple Sophie. And who is this?"

"Allow me, Your Majesty!" Benjamin Franklin strolled into the square with Bancroft. "This boy is my servant, Emile. A fine lad."

"Well, he appears suitably shabby. He may stay."

"Er, thank you, my Queen," said Emile.

"Your Majesty, will you please tell me about this . . . display," said Franklin with a smile.

"Do you like it? Trianon is my private haven. I do so like the simplicity of the common peasant. They require so little and yet are so very content!"

"Hmm," said Franklin. "A very well-designed square."

"Thank you," said Marie Antoinette. "I designed it myself with some help from Monsieur Montgolfier. Such a clever fellow. He insisted on personally overseeing the construction of the buildings, particularly the barn," she said with a slightly perplexed look. "I suppose he is very fond of barns."

"Who is not?" Franklin smiled. "And what a fine barn."

"Yes, and you *must* see this!" The queen skipped over to the barnyard. The others followed.

"Voilà!" said Marie Antoinette, gesturing toward Pierre, Bernadette, and Jean-Luc.

"Oh, animals, too," said Franklin.

"Not just any farm animals, my dear Benjamin," said the queen, bursting with pride. "Famous animals!"

"You don't say," indulged Franklin.

"I do say. These are the same sheep, rooster, and duck that flew in the Montgolfiers' marvelous balloon."

"Quack," said Jean-Luc.

"How marvelous indeed!" called out a deep, rumbling voice.

Everyone turned to see a tall man approaching the barn. He wore all black, including a flowing black cloak.

"Cagliostro!" said Marie Antoinette with a beaming smile. "You scoundrel. Always sneaking up on me."

"I could not decline your kind invitation to visit the

famous Trianon," said Cagliostro with a deep bow. His eyes scanned the animals.

"Do you know the great Cagliostro?" Marie Antoinette asked Franklin. "He is quite the celebrity. A most amazing man!"

"Count Cagliostro!" Bancroft stepped forward and bowed.

"Ah, Bancroft. How is your dear fiancée in England?" asked Cagliostro with a warm smile.

"Well, thank you," said Bancroft. "I owe her a letter. Perhaps this week," he added with what Emile thought was a wink.

"I do not believe I have had the pleasure," said Franklin.

"Nor I," said Cagliostro. "It is an honor to meet the distinguished inventor, Benjamin Franklin."

"You have heard of my tinkering?" asked Franklin.

"Of course," said Cagliostro, smiling. "I keep up

with all of the innovations of this age."

"He knows everything," gushed the queen. "He is much, much older than he appears."

"Three thousand and two years old," said Cagliostro modestly. "Three thousand and three next May."

"My," said Franklin. "You look so young. Do tell me your secret."

"Sorcery. Also, abstaining from red meat."

Pierre flapped his wings and hopped onto a water barrel.

Cagliostro turned and took a step closer to Bernadette. "The famous sheep, rooster, and duck. I have heard *so* much about them. *ACHOO!*"

Cagliostro pulled out a black handkerchief. "Do excuse me."

"Three thousand years of suffering from allergies. How vexing," said Franklin.

"You sound as if you doubt my age," Cagliostro said with a grin.

"As a man of science, I must scoff at the idea," said Franklin.

"Tut, tut. You must keep an open mind, Monsieur Franklin."

"My mind is open to science."

"Boys, boys," laughed the queen. "Let us not bicker in simple, happy Trianon. This is a place of joy, the joy of making do with the hardy staples of an uncomplicated life."

"Pfft," said Sophie.

"What was that, Sophie?" asked the queen.

"Time to feed the animals, my Queen. Would you like to scatter the meal?"

"Oh, heavens, no. You go on, dear peasant."

"I am afraid that I must take my leave," said Franklin. "The king has requested a special service from me tonight. I must plan with my team."

Franklin turned to Emile.

"I do not seem to recall you arriving with us. Do you need a ride back?"

"No, sir," said Emile. "I rode Fifi."

"Fine. I shall see you back at Passy."

"Then I shall see you tonight, Monsieur Franklin,"

said Cagliostro. "At Franz Mesmer's salon, will I not?"

Franklin stared at Cagliostro. "How did you know that the king wished me to visit Herr Mesmer?"

Cagliostro chuckled.

"You see!" exclaimed the queen. "Sorcerer! He is full of tricks."

"I imagine he is. Until tonight, Mr. Cagliostro. Thank you, Your Majesty, for the delightful tour." Franklin bowed, and he, Bancroft, and Emile departed. Emile waved at Sophie.

Sophie scattered the meal into the pen without a glance at Emile.

"And now, my dear Cagliostro, you must tell me of your latest adventures. Perhaps you would enjoy visiting the candle shoppe?"

"Nothing would give me more pleasure, Your Majesty."

Marie Antoinette skipped off across the square. Before joining her, Cagliostro took one more long look at the barnyard.

The sheep, rooster, and duck stared back.

Cagliostro began to whistle and followed the queen.

~⊘ Chapter Seven ⊘~

$\mathcal{B}$enjamin Franklin sat in his parlor with a very pleased smile.

"Emile, tonight will be fun," Franklin said, closing his eyes as though savoring the thought.

"Monsieur?" Emile set a tray of cheese and bread on a side table.

"There is a new charlatan in town. One Franz Mesmer, who claims to be a hypnotist. He has convinced half of Paris that he possesses immense powers and can cure the afflicted mind through his animal magnetism."

"Animal magnetism?"

"That is what he calls it. He claims to tap into unseen forces within the human mind using a special machine. It is, as we say in Philadelphia, codswallop."

"Cod—?"

"Hooey. A bucket of it," said Franklin.

"And you are attending Monsieur Mesmer's salon tonight to prove him a fraud," said Emile.

"Exactly. But the best part, Emile, is that I shall not be alone." Franklin nibbled some cheese. "I shall be assisted by Antoine Lavoisier, noted chemist, and Joseph Guillotin, who is about as sharp a fellow as you are to find in Paris."

A knock sounded from the front door.

"They have arrived!" Franklin rose and hurried to the door. Before opening it, he paused and looked at Emile.

"There is nothing better than a real team!"

Franklin opened the door wide to greet Lavoisier and Guillotin.

Emile prepared a second tray of cheese for the guests and drifted out of the salon so the team could plan the evening ahead.

It was a good opportunity to change the linens, so Emile gathered fresh sheets and climbed the stairs. He paused.

Bancroft stood outside Monsieur Franklin's study, quietly jiggling the doorknob.

"The study is locked," said Emile.

Bancroft's eyes flashed with anger. He took a breath, and something approximating a smile slithered across his face.

"Yes, of course," said Bancroft.

"Shall I ask Monsieur Franklin for the key?" asked Emile.

"No. It is nothing." Bancroft stepped casually away from the door.

"Monsieur Franklin thought it best to keep his study—and his notebook—safe," said Emile.

"Franklin thought of that, did he?" Bancroft loomed over Emile.

"I may have suggested it," said Emile. He was suddenly very aware of his precarious position at the top of the stairs.

"How . . . helpful." Bancroft's voice was low and dangerous.

Emile waited. Bancroft said no more, but continued staring at him.

"Is there anything else I can do for you, Monsieur Bancroft?"

"You have done quite enough, boy."

Emile bowed his head and scooted around Bancroft toward the bedroom.

"Boy," called Bancroft from the stairs.

Emile turned back.

"Know your place."

"*Oui*, Monsieur," said Emile quietly.

Bancroft turned and descended the stairs.

Emile exhaled. He glanced once more at the locked study, then entered the bedroom with the fresh sheets gripped tightly in his hands.

👁 👁 👁

Meanwhile, in the secret headquarters below the

Trianon barn, another team was also making plans for the evening.

"Emile is essential," said the duck, tapping a floor plan of Mesmer's house.

"Can we trust him?" asked Sophie. "His loyalty is to Franklin. Also, he seems a bit dim."

"Oh, I don't know, Sophie," said Pierre, donning his mask. "He followed little Felix here and discovered our headquarters. Not bad, I say."

"And he will surely be with Monsieur Franklin at Mesmer's salon," added Bernadette. "*Inside* the house. His eyes could be our eyes."

"Unless you would like to reconsider my other strategy," said Jean-Luc.

"I will not pose as an ottoman," said the sheep with dignity.

"Very well," said the duck. "But we're not ruling that

out for the future. It's too good an idea."

"*I* could be on the inside," said Sophie. "Being human and all."

"You are not a known servant, my dear. Emile has the perfect job. Besides," the rooster continued as he tied his sash and checked his sword, "Emile will not be completely alone. I will be lurking in the shadows, as usual."

"Quietly," stressed Bernadette. "This is an ideal opportunity to learn more about Cagliostro's plans. We do not need fancy swashbuckling tonight, Pierre."

"Oh, Bernadette. You love danger when up in a balloon; why so cautious on terra firma?" said Pierre.

"Bernadette is right. Stick to the plan," said Jean-Luc.

"I shall not buckle a single swash," said the rooster solemnly. "Unless someone else starts something."

"I suppose that's the best we can expect of you." Bernadette sighed. "Sophie, if you would be so kind as

to bring around the carriage, we will be off. Felix, watch over headquarters. There's cheese in the cupboard, dear."

The mouse floated lazily across the room in his tiny balloon. He gave a thumbs-up.

~ Chapter Eight ~

$\mathcal{E}$veryone who was *anyone* was in attendance at that night's salon. Franz Mesmer was a sensation. Visiting from his native Austria, Mesmer had been captivating the well-to-do with demonstrations of his unique machine and marvelous powers. They had even coined a new word to describe his effect on his subjects. They were *mesmerized*.

Mesmer claimed, and often demonstrated, his power to cure ailments, adjust attitudes, and even convince those under his spell that they were animals. He called the property that he manipulated "animal magnetism," an invisible force that flows through all.

Yet not all were convinced that Mesmer was a legitimate and good addition to society. And that was why the king had sent Benjamin Franklin to the salon this fateful night.

Emile had been directed to the kitchen to offer his assistance to the household staff. The head butler was a large, grumpy man. He examined Emile's clothing and general appearance.

"We are short one servant tonight. You will do. First, go make sure the horses are tied securely, then return to the salon. Speak only when spoken to. Can you carry a tray?"

"Yes, Monsieur," said Emile.

"Fine," said the butler. "Go, go!"

Emile rushed through the kitchen and into the yard. Carriages were lined up properly. The horses were watered and fed. The drivers congregated nearby. All was in order. He returned to the kitchen.

"Psst!"

Emile froze. He looked around. No one was there.

"Up," said a whisper.

There, suspended upside down, was Pierre the rooster.

"Oh, hello," said Emile.

"Fine evening, is it not?" asked Pierre.

"Yes," said Emile. "I guess."

"I just wanted you to know that I am here, but you are the eyes on the inside, Emile. Keep close watch on Franklin, Mesmer, and especially Cagliostro. Let me know if anything unusual occurs. I will be in the shadows."

"But—Pierre—" Emile started.

"Don't worry, Emile," said Pierre. "You are going to be fine."

Emile gulped and made his way inside. The salon was in full swing.

Strangely beautiful music came from the corner. A man in a tinted wig and very fine clothing was playing a musical instrument that Emile had never seen before. It was made primarily of glass. The musician's skill was something to behold. His hands were everywhere at once.

Benjamin Franklin and his team had gathered around the musician.

"What a pleasure it is to hear the famed Mozart play the glass armonica," said Franklin. "Do you like the instrument, sir?"

Mozart looked up with an expression of manic glee. "I adore it!" exclaimed Mozart. His every word and

movement seemed punctuated by an exclamation point. "Do you play?!"

"I have dabbled," said Franklin.

"He has done significantly more than dabble, dear Mozart." A tall, slender man dressed in elegant lavender silks joined the group. His eyes were a most piercing blue. "In fact, Benjamin Franklin invented the glass armonica."

"No!" said Mozart. "Really?!"

"I tinker," said Franklin.

"Are all Americans so modest?" said the slender man.

"I do not believe we have been introduced. I am Franz Mesmer."

"Charmed to make your acquaintance," said Franklin.

"*Charmed?*" asked Mesmer. "Are you truly?"

"A figure of speech," said Franklin. "These are my associates, Monsieur Lavoisier and Monsieur Guillotin."

The gentlemen nodded.

"Welcome, all," said Mesmer.

"I understand that you are an inventor as well, Herr Mesmer," said Franklin with a polite smile.

"I suppose you would like to see a demonstration of my apparatus," said Mesmer with an equally polite smile.

"Indeed," said Franklin. "I have heard so much about your . . . animal . . . what is it again?"

"Animal magnetism!" shouted Mozart, adding a spooky flourish of notes on the glass armonica. "Franz Mesmer! Is! Brilliant! He made me quite believe I was a chicken at the last salon!"

"You will make me blush, dear Wolfgang," said Mesmer. "I would be happy to demonstrate. I am simply waiting for *all* my guests to arrive."

A gasp rippled through the room. All heads turned to the entrance. There stood Cagliostro, cloak swirling around him.

"Oooooooh," murmured the crowd.

Emile gulped quietly.

"Thank you," said Cagliostro. "Good evening to you all."

"Cagliostro, my dear friend. Welcome!" said Mesmer.

Cagliostro crossed the room.

"I would say that I hope I am not late, but, of course, I know I was destined to arrive exactly on time," laughed Cagliostro.

"He can tell the future!" blurted an excited gentlewoman.

"You are too kind, Madame." Cagliostro bowed. "And fortunate for all, your kindness will continue to touch friends and family for exactly thirty-seven more years."

"Oh." The woman counted in her head. "At my age, that means . . . well, that is fine." She blushed.

"Before you start telling everyone's fortune," interrupted Franklin, "Herr Mesmer has agreed to demonstrate his animal magnetism."

"Wonderful!" said Cagliostro. "I do revere science."

Cagliostro took a seat on a chaise lounge between

Madame du Barry and Madame Moreau.

"Please proceed," said Cagliostro.

"Mr. Franklin, if you and your associates would follow me," said Mesmer.

Emile craned his neck to see through the guests. Franklin and the others gathered around a strange contraption. It had large vials of liquid, glass tubes, copper orbs, and various handles arranged in a circle.

"Please, if you would each place your hands on the conductivity poles," said Mesmer. "There is nothing to fear."

"We are not afraid," said Guillotin.

They did as Mesmer asked.

The machine began to hum.

Mesmer drew a metal wand from inside his coat pocket.

"A magic wand, Mesmer?" asked Franklin. "How surprising."

"This wand is merely a conducive device, a way for me to draw out the magnetic fluids present in your corporeal self."

"Oh," said Franklin. "I thought you were going to produce a rabbit."

Emile chuckled, along with a few of the guests.

"Now, please relax," said Mesmer, lifting his wand. His blue eyes bored into his subjects. A hush fell over the salon. Only the gentle hum of the apparatus could be heard.

Mesmer began to murmur a string of words very low. Emile could not make out what he was saying.

Liquid in the vials began to bubble. The room seemed to grow very warm and stuffy.

Lavoisier began to perspire. He swayed slightly.

Mesmer stood before Franklin. Franklin stared into those piercing blue eyes.

"You, Benjamin Franklin," whispered Mesmer. "You . . . are . . . a . . . *chicken.*"

The room held its breath. Emile leaned in to get a better view. Cagliostro watched with his dark, unblinking eyes.

Franklin remained perfectly still.

"In my country, we prefer the turkey," said Franklin with a smile.

Mesmer lowered his wand. "My error." He grinned and bowed slightly.

The audience began to whisper among themselves.

"I am afraid, my society friends," said Franklin in a loud, clear voice, "that mesmerism is merely the power of suggestion. It will only work if the subject truly believes that Franz Mesmer is a hypnotist. I would suggest that Mesmer is no more than a charlatan!"

"BA-GOCK!"

Mozart pecked at the buffet table, clucking contentedly.

Mesmer laughed. "Perhaps not, Mr. Franklin."

The crowd chuckled nervously. Emile tensed, eyes on Franklin.

"And what have you against charlatans?" boomed Cagliostro from his chaise. "Charlatans throughout history have, in many cases, *made* history."

"But never for the better," said Franklin.

"Please, Monsieur Franklin," pleaded an older gentleman. "Do not anger Cagliostro. He is a sorcerer!"

"He is a fraud," stated Franklin.

Silence fell in the room.

"Ladies and gentlemen," Cagliostro purred with a grin. "I present to you Benjamin Franklin . . . a true Man of Enlightenment."

Cagliostro clapped his hands, and the entire room fell into complete and utter darkness.

Chapter Nine

$\mathcal{M}$esmer's servants rushed in to light the candles as the guests tittered, objected, and, in a few cases, fainted. Emile made his way to the center of the room as the candlelight brought the surroundings slowly into view.

Benjamin Franklin, Lavoisier, and Guillotin were gone. Emile scoured the room in a panic. Cagliostro and Mesmer were also missing.

Emile shoved through the guests, into the kitchen and out the back door.

He collided with a tall figure in a black cloak.

"Well, now," said Cagliostro. "What have we here? Franklin's servant."

He grabbed Emile by the arm with a vise-like grip.

"You may prove useful."

"I *do* hate to go back on a promise," said a voice from the shadows. "But you most certainly have started something."

Pierre leaped gracefully down onto a barrel, sword raised.

"Finally," said Cagliostro, "we truly meet."

"I have indeed been looking forward to this, Cagliostro," said Pierre. "Let the boy go."

"Of course," said Cagliostro, releasing Emile. In the same motion he drew his sword from under his cloak. "One moment, please." He dug into another pocket and produced the birdlike mask.

"It would not be fair if you were the *only* one in a mask. You don't mind?"

"Actually, that makes this even easier," said Pierre.

Cagliostro lunged, and the rooster met his blade. Emile took cover as the duel commenced, equal parts nervous and entertained by the masterful fencing that now played before his eyes.

"I would love to continue this to its inevitable end," said Cagliostro.

"Am I keeping you?" asked Pierre, parrying a thrust.

"As a matter of fact, you are," said Cagliostro. "But I am sure we shall meet again quite soon."

Cagliostro threw something to the ground and a bright light flashed, followed by a plume of white smoke.

When it cleared, Cagliostro had vanished.

"Parlor tricks," said Pierre. "Typical. Are you all right, Emile?"

"Yes, but they've taken Monsieur Franklin!"

"I know. There is no more we can do here. We must rendezvous with the others."

Minutes later they were inside the team's sleek black carriage. Emile filled in Bernadette, Jean-Luc, Sophie, and Pierre on everything he had witnessed at the salon.

"They will be long gone by now," said Jean-Luc. "I suggest we return to headquarters and discuss strategy."

All agreed this was the best course of action (Emile, reluctantly). Back at Trianon, the five sat around the workbench in silence. Emile slumped on his stool.

"Do cheer up, Emile. All is not lost," said Bernadette. "This is only a setback, not an end."

Emile looked down.

Sophie nudged him. "You are with *the* sheep, rooster, and duck. Do you have any idea what they are capable of? What they have done in the past?"

Sophie stood.

"Now, Sophie," said Bernadette. "We don't need to go into all that. . . . "

"After the balloon flight," continued Sophie, "they didn't just retire to a quiet barnyard. They spread throughout France, each contributing to society with their talents."

She gestured to the duck, who was moving small figures on a map.

"Take Jean-Luc. He first volunteered his services to the French navy as a tactician."

"A duck does take to water," said Jean-Luc, without looking up.

"Then there is Pierre!" continued Sophie.

"I thought you would have begun with my tale, but go ahead," said the rooster.

Bête Noire

"And last, but certainly not least . . . Bernadette!"

"I think Emile has the idea, dear."

"The Montgolfier balloon was very, very good. But Bernadette pushed them to do better. And now, her unparalleled inventions are the most exquisite vessels in the air!"

"I was inspired, Emile. My good friend and partner Monsieur Montgolfier called balloons a 'cloud in a paper bag.' I always rather liked that phrase. And do you know what he called the special property in the smoke that lifts the balloon?"

"What?" asked Emile.

"Levity. Lightheartedness."

Bernadette gazed at her designs hanging on the walls.

"Through plague and war, poverty, desperation, crime—all of it—there is still art, Emile. Wonder casts a spell over all living creatures, great and small. Just look at the skies at night and imagine what could be. Art, science, imagination . . . all create wonder."

Emile joined her and admired her watercolor paintings.

"So you see," said Sophie. "On your side is the most extraordinary team in France. Or the world."

"For now, let us sleep," said Jean-Luc. "We need rest to live up to the legend."

~ Chapter Ten ~

The next morning, Emile returned to Passy alone. Bernadette, Jean-Luc, and Pierre assured him that they would find Franklin, but Emile was tasked with protecting Franklin's notebook. He hurried into the house and up the stairs, sick with worry. What if they never found—

"Monsieur Franklin!" exclaimed Emile.

Benjamin Franklin sat at his desk in the study. He did not turn around.

"Emile? Where have you been? I was most worried."

"But . . . you . . . I . . . " sputtered Emile.

"I was worried *and* famished, I must admit," said Franklin with a chuckle. "I do believe I must keep up my nutrition. I seem to be getting forgetful. I can't quite recall how I returned home last night."

He closed his notebook and stood with a beaming smile.

"No matter! Now, how about breakfast?"

He walked past Emile, who still stood by the door, mouth agape.

"Last night, Monsieur Franklin," said Emile, hurrying to follow. "You . . . where did you . . . "

Franklin entered the kitchen. "Do we still have some of that lovely bread? And eggs this morning would be nice."

There was a knock at the front door.

"Answer that, will you?" said Franklin, humming to himself and slicing some bread.

Emile backed down the hall toward the door, still speaking. "What happened last night with Herr Mesmer and . . . "

Emile opened the door.

"Cagliostro."

"Hello again." Cagliostro stood on the doorstep with a sly grin.

"Who is it?" asked Franklin from the hall. He stopped and stared.

"Cagliostro, my friend!" he exclaimed.

"You old so-and-so! What brings you by?"

Cagliostro swept past Emile.

"Just in the area, my dear Franklin. Thought I would pop in for a visit!"

"Wonderful! Wonderful! Have a seat. Emile, close the door."

Emile closed the door slowly, his eyes locked on Cagliostro.

Franklin and Cagliostro sat down in the parlor, grinning at each other.

"Well, well," said Cagliostro.

"Well, well, well," rejoined Franklin.

"Quite a salon last night, wouldn't you say?" asked Cagliostro.

"Simply splendid!" said Franklin. "Utterly fascinating."

Emile hovered outside the parlor.

"How did you sleep?" asked Cagliostro.

"Like a baby," said Franklin. "Woke up refreshed and energized. I seem to be full of new ideas! My pen could barely keep up with my brain as I scribbled in my notebook."

"Marvelous," said Cagliostro. "I would love to see that old notebook of yours."

Emile, hidden in the hall, held his breath.

Franklin's smile faded a bit. He shook his head.

"Oh, no. I *am* sorry, but there are some inventions in there that I . . . I shouldn't share. Purely theoretical, you know."

"Still, I would be most interested to see how that amazing brain of yours works."

"I simply couldn't, my dear friend," said Franklin.

"I completely understand," said Cagliostro. "Well, I must be off."

"So soon?" said Franklin. "We were about to make breakfast."

"Things to do, my friend," said Cagliostro, rising.

"Of course," said Franklin. "I imagine your day is quite full."

Cagliostro paused at the door.

"Perhaps you would like to visit me later at my secret society?" asked Cagliostro.

"Which secret society is yours? Illuminate Enigma? Society of Cosmic Confluence? Not the Freemasons?"

"The Rosicrucian Society of Universal Harmony," said Cagliostro.

"Oh, I've heard that is a good one," said Franklin.

"It is quite extraordinary," said Cagliostro. "We

have a simply amazing chef. He can do wonders with . . . *mayonnaise.*"

Franklin stiffened slightly. His eyes seemed to glaze over.

" . . . Mayonnaise?"

"Mayonnaise," repeated Cagliostro in a low voice.

MAY-O-NNAISE

"May . . . o . . . nnaise," whispered Franklin. "Yes, of course. Excellent."

"Shall we say six o'clock?" said Cagliostro.

"Six o'clock," repeated Franklin.

"Adieu, my dear friend." Cagliostro swept out the front door, letting it close behind him.

Franklin remained in exactly the same spot, staring at the door.

"Monsieur Franklin," Emile said tentatively, entering the parlor.

"I am not to be disturbed today, Emile. I have much work to do in my study."

Franklin moved past Emile without a glance and started up the stairs.

"Shall I bring you breakfast?" asked Emile.

"I shall eat later. Six o'clock. Mayonnaise."

Franklin entered his study and shut the door.

Emile had no idea what
to do.

Squeak!

Felix the mouse was on
the windowsill. He sat in
the basket of a tiny
balloon. The balloon
was shaped like a wedge
of cheese.

Felix beckoned.

Emile walked over. The mouse held out a small scrap
of paper.

"Stick by Franklin," read Emile.

The boy nodded to the mouse. Felix opened a tiny
valve at the base of the balloon. It lifted into the air and
sailed off. The cheese wedge design seemed built for
speed.

Emile watched the mouse fly away. He exhaled. He would stick by Monsieur Franklin. But would that be enough?

~Chapter Eleven~

$\mathcal{B}$enjamin Franklin worked at his desk all day long. Emile offered food and drink, but Franklin refused. Sweeping in the study was not even a remote possibility.

Emile fretted. He cleaned. He cleaned and cleaned. When all was thoroughly spotless, Emile took a short break. Though satisfying as always, cleaning had not eased his mind. Emile decided to do the one thing that always calmed him down.

He began to draw. He drew the sheep. He drew the

soufflé balloon. He drew Felix the mouse. He even drew Sophie. She would probably hate the idea of him drawing her, he thought. Still, it was an excellent likeness.

Emile became so caught up in his drawing that he did not hear Franklin approach the kitchen.

"Please prepare the carriage," said Franklin.

"But, Monsieur Franklin, I thought your appointment was at six," said Emile desperately.

"It is. However, I am not entirely sure of the precise location of Cagliostro's society. There are several on Secret Society Boulevard. It may take some time to find the correct one."

"Yes, sir."

Emile reluctantly prepared the carriage and horse. He worked slowly but not too slowly. His professionalism would not allow that. He finished his task and hitched the horse to the rail in front of the house.

"That will be all, boy."

Emile turned. Edward Bancroft approached the carriage.

"I must drive the carriage," said Emile. "Monsieur Franklin is going to meet with—"

"*Cagliostro*. Yes. I am fully aware of the situation. *I* will make absolutely sure that Franklin and Count Cagliostro keep their appointment."

"Oh," said Emile. He didn't like the hint of reverence in Bancroft's voice as he said Cagliostro's name. And how would he be able to stick with Monsieur Franklin if Bancroft drove the carriage?

Benjamin Franklin appeared from the house. He climbed into the carriage, then patted his pockets with mild annoyance.

"Oh, dear! What *is* the matter with my memory? I have forgotten the most important thing. Emile," he called, "please go to my study and retrieve my notebook."

"Your notebook?" asked Emile. "But Monsieur Franklin . . . you have never taken that outside the study."

"You heard your master," said Bancroft. "Fetch the notebook. Now."

Emile hurried into the house, up the stairs, and into the study. There was the notebook, lying open on the desk.

Emile stared at the page. Franklin had added new, detailed sketches and notes for the Heat Ray. The design was complete. *Operational* was noted at the bottom of the page. Emile placed a finger on the diagram for the lethal device. He glanced at

Franklin's quill pen, still wet with ink.

"What took you so long?" demanded Bancroft when Emile emerged with the notebook.

Emile held up a box tied with a string. "Bread and cheese for the journey," he said.

"Oh," said Franklin. "Yes. I *am* peckish actually."

"There will be food at the secret society," said Bancroft. "Mayo—"

"Maybe not!" burst Emile. "You can never tell with secret societies."

"True," said Franklin. "You know, Emile, with my memory issues of late, it might be best if you came along. You are always so on top of things."

Emile climbed into the carriage under a glare from Bancroft.

"HIYAH!" barked Bancroft, and the carriage set off down the road.

Emile's mind raced. He was still with Franklin. That was good. Bancroft was driving the carriage. That was bad. Franklin still seemed slightly dazed. That was very bad. Franklin was bringing his notebook to Cagliostro. That was very, very bad. One good, three bad. Emile did not like the odds of this turning out well.

"Whoa!" called Bancroft. The carriage came to a halt. "What is the meaning of this?"

Emile looked out of the window. Another carriage was blocking the road, and a gentleman was slowly disembarking.

The man ignored Bancroft and approached the carriage. He smiled.

"Bonjour, Monsieur Franklin!"

"Oh, hello," said Franklin. "It's . . . I am sorry. I have forgotten your name."

"Montgolfier."

"Yes! The balloon man!"

"My company manufactures balloons, yes," said Montgolfier. "I thought I recognized your carriage."

"Are you going to a secret society, too?" asked Franklin.

Montgolfier chuckled. "Oh, no. Too stuffy, those places. I prefer fresh air. I am off to the exposition."

"What exposition?" asked Franklin.

"Why, the lighter-than-air balloon exposition! It's today! Just there, over the hill. Would you care to join me?"

"Mr. Franklin," said Bancroft, "I am afraid we do not have time for frivolity."

"Surely there is always time for marvels," said Montgolfier. "If I recall, you are quite an admirer."

"I am indeed," said Franklin. His gaze was clearer than Emile had seen it all day.

"And I have never seen a balloon launch," added Emile quickly. "Oh, but forgive me. I shouldn't have spoken. I was just so excited."

"As well you should be, my boy," said Montgolfier. "Today we have some splendid new designs. State of the art."

"That does sound intriguing," said Franklin. "I was not aware of this event."

"It was scheduled quite recently," said Montgolfier. He winked at Emile.

Franklin thought for a moment.

"Yes. Yes, we can spare one hour, surely."

"But, Mr. Franklin—" Bancroft began.

"Allow me to escort you in my carriage," interrupted Montgolfier. "I know the way."

"Thank you," said Franklin. "Come along, Emile. Bring the cheese."

Emile had not noticed how beautiful the day was until they crested the hill and beheld a field of breathtaking balloons against the green grass and clear blue sky.

Each balloon was intricately painted. The baskets were finely made in a variety of sizes and levels of comfort.

Strong ropes tethered the marvels to the ground, but each balloon strained to rise up to where it truly belonged.

"Monsieur Franklin, here is my latest balloon. A collaboration, really," said Montgolfier. "May I introduce the aeronaut?"

"Sophie!" exclaimed Emile.

Sophie stood before the most elaborate and impressive of the balloons. She had her hands on her hips and wore men's breeches and boots. She exuded calm, cool confidence.

"So young a pilot," said Franklin.

"Sophie is incredibly skilled," said Montgolfier. "And utterly fearless."

"Montgolfier!" A cheerful gentleman approached. "Beautiful work, as usual."

"Thank you, Dr. Charles," said Montgolfier. "Monsieur Franklin, may I present Dr. Alexander Charles, one of our most enthusiastic aeronauts."

"Monsieur Franklin! A pleasure. Are you ascending today?"

"Goodness, no," said Franklin. "I am merely an observer."

"You are missing out. Nothing will ever quite equal the moment of total hilarity that filled my whole body at

takeoff. How are you, Sophie? Conditions right?"

"Conditions excellent," said Sophie.

"I agree. Now, none of your tricks and fancy stunts today. You make the rest of us look bad." The gentleman smiled broadly. "My, it was a surprise to hear of this sudden launch. But any launch is a good launch!"

"And we should launch soon," said Sophie.

"Yes, we are only waiting on a delivery of cold chicken and champagne," said Dr. Charles. "We simply must have the proper sustenance, Monsieur Franklin. We never launch without cold chicken and champagne."

"Pfft," said Sophie.

"Also," continued Dr. Charles, "there was a change in aeronaut for . . . balloon twelve. Yes. Should be ready to go in a moment."

Emile and Sophie looked across the field at balloon twelve.

Amid some commotion, a rider on a black horse was arriving beside Bancroft. He dismounted with a flourish of cape. Cagliostro!

"Monsieur Franklin," said Sophie quickly. "Are you sure you would not like to see the inside of the basket?"

She opened the door to the spacious basket. Cabinets were built into the wicker of the sides. "We have many scientific instruments on board."

"Do you?" asked Franklin, approaching. He peered inside the basket.

"*Pardonez-moi,*"
said Sophie, and she
shoved Benjamin Franklin
into the basket. She jumped in and
shut the door.

"LAUNCH!" she called, throwing a
lever. A blast of fire shot up into the balloon.
Montgolfier pulled up the stakes. Emile tried to help, but
as the balloon lifted, his leg tangled in ropes and up he
went with it.

"Sophie!" he called out.

Across the field, all had turned to watch. Cagliostro climbed into the basket of balloon twelve.

"AWAY!" he bellowed.

Emile managed to grab hold of the rope and Sophie and Franklin pulled him aboard. He looked down. This was a mistake. He nearly fainted as he watched the ground fall away.

"This is very distressing," said Franklin. "Miss, kindly return to the ground."

"I'm afraid I cannot do that at this time," said Sophie as she dropped various sandbags overboard.

The other balloons had launched and most were slowly drifting upward. Balloon twelve, however, was ascending rapidly. Emile and Sophie could clearly see Cagliostro in the basket, blasting fire into the balloon.

"We have company," announced Sophie.

The cabinet doors in the basket slid open, and Bernadette, Pierre, and Jean-Luc emerged. Jean-Luc trained a spyglass on balloon twelve.

"He knows what he is doing," said Jean-Luc. "Impressive."

"He's no Sophie," said Pierre.

"Of course not," said Bernadette. "Sophie, we may need to push the limits today. Are you ready?"

"*Oui*, Bernadette," said Sophie, with a grin. "Sounds like fun."

Emile was relieved to have the sheep, rooster, and duck aboard. He looked over at Benjamin Franklin to see his reaction.

Franklin stared at the animals.

"Hello, Monsieur Franklin," said Bernadette. "Welcome to the heavens."

Franklin sat down in the basket. "Emile, I think I

might be experiencing some mild hallucinations."

"Would you like some bread and cheese?" asked Bernadette.

"No," said Franklin vaguely. "I am . . . saving my appetite for . . . mayonnaise."

Franklin's eyes glazed over and he passed out cold.

"It seems the change of altitude has affected Monsieur Franklin," said Jean-Luc. "It is probably for the best. Pierre, where is Cagliostro?"

"Closer than I would like," called Pierre from the ropes.

Bernadette and Sophie tended to the fire. The balloon ascended rapidly to a great height, high above the others. They were now in the clouds. All was white.

And then, suddenly, Cagliostro's balloon emerged like the fin of a shark. In a moment he rose to their altitude.

"Right," said Bernadette. "We shall see about this."

I can't see him.

There! Below us!

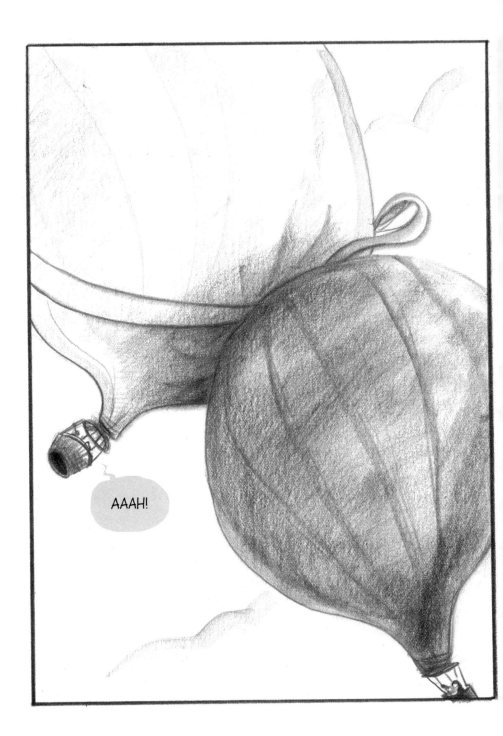

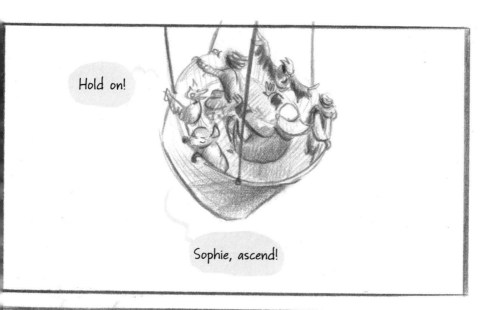

Here he comes!

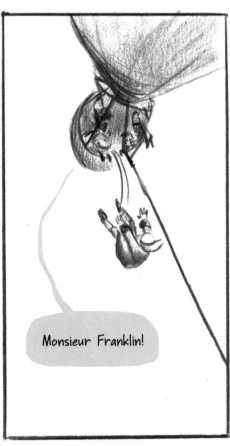

Monsieur Franklin!

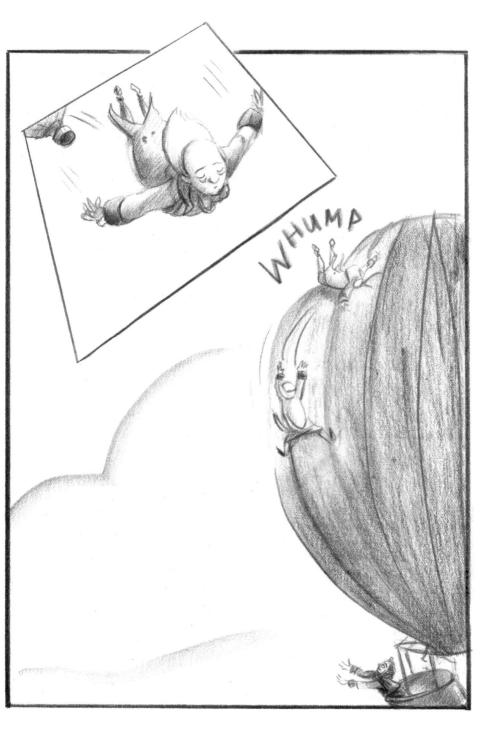

WHUMP

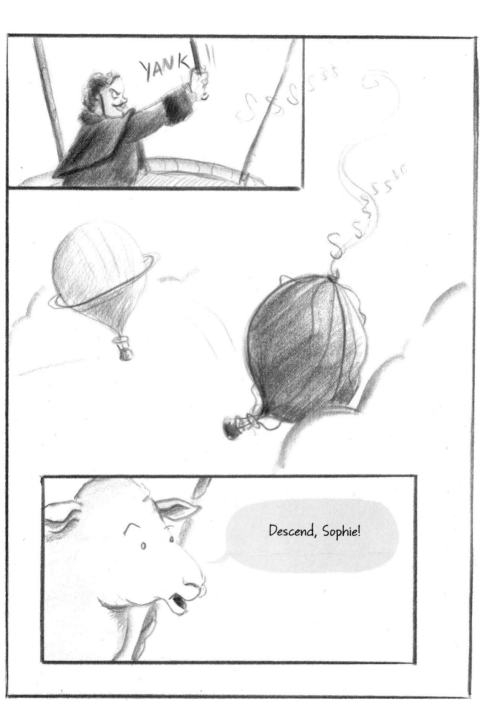

~⌾ Chapter Twelve ⌾~

$\mathcal{B}$ack at the secret headquarters beneath the barn, our heroes gathered around the worktable. They were down, but not beaten.

"So," Bernadette began, "Cagliostro has Benjamin Franklin."

"He has procured Franklin's notebook and, thus, his plans for various weaponry," added Pierre.

"And he has injured the pride of one duck," said Jean-Luc. "This puts him far across the line."

"Do not act from anger or pride, Jean-Luc," cautioned Bernadette. "That is much too human. No offense," she said to Sophie and Emile.

"No offense taken," said Sophie. "I am personally ashamed of the depths my species is capable of plumbing."

"We must rescue Monsieur Franklin," said Emile. "He is not a bad man. And he never intended for those plans to be seen, let alone used."

"We shall rescue him, Emile," assured Pierre. "Never fear. We know our next step."

"Here," said Bernadette, pointing to a map on the table. The map showed a small village on the outskirts of Paris.

"The Boulevard of Secret Societies," said Jean-Luc. "This is where we will find Cagliostro."

"The Rosicru . . . Rosicru-something society?"

"That is what Cagliostro *said*, but the Rosicrucian Society of Universal Harmony closed due to excessive rat infestation. We believe Cagliostro instructed the spy Bancroft to deliver Franklin to his *true* secret society."

"Which one?" asked Emile.

"We have narrowed it down," said Jean-Luc. The duck pointed to three buildings. "This is the Fabulist Society of Ancient Mysteries, here is the Skull and Bones and More Skulls Society, and here is the Mystic Order of the Enchanted Moose."

"Is it one of those?" asked Emile.

"No, of course not. Those are the most ridiculous ones," said Jean-Luc. "Granted, the bar is rather low."

"What about these three?" asked Sophie, pointing to three adjacent buildings at the end of the road.

"Yes, those are mysteries even to us," said Bernadette. "Cagliostro must be in one of them."

"And so that is where we will find Monsieur Franklin," said Emile.

"Assuredly," said the duck.

"Three societies and three of us," said Pierre.

"Wait a minute, Pierre," said Sophie. "You are not suggesting I stay here with the boy?"

"We're the same age, you know," mumbled Emile.

"This is too dangerous, Sophie. We must move swiftly and undetected. We will determine the correct society, regroup, and move in with full force," said Bernadette.

"Until then, we need you and Emile here," said Pierre.

"Safe and ready for whatever comes next," said Jean-Luc.

"That sounds reasonable," said Emile.

"I do not like it," said Sophie.

"It is the best strategy," said Jean-Luc. "And not up for a vote."

Bernadette patted Sophie's hand. "I know it is frustrating. But look on the bright side: we will need to go at night, with great speed and stealth."

Sophie looked up with a gleam in her eye.

"You mean . . . the night gliders?"

"Our latest creation," smiled Bernadette.

"I do hope this one comes with seat belts," said Jean-Luc.

~ Chapter Thirteen ~

$\mathcal{B}$ernadette made her way down a spiral staircase. All was quiet and still. At the foot of the stairs was a single white door. She peered through the keyhole, then opened the door.

The next room was candlelit, and the walls were painted a warm yellow. Shelves held fabrics of every shade and pattern. Long worktables stood with well-organized racks of scissors, tapes, and chalk. Beautiful and unusual clothing designs were displayed on wooden easels.

The room led into a hallway lined with the most wonderful gowns, suits, and hats. Bernadette admired each one.

Another staircase brought her to a different workspace. The tables here held an array of the most marvelous mechanical toys, each more intricate than the last.

Bernadette could not help but touch one. A flock of miniature sheep stood in a tiny meadow. At her touch, the meadow began to revolve slowly and the sheep sang a charming melody, their mechanical mouths opening in time.

Bernadette glanced around the room. She was alone, and the music had not alerted anyone to her presence. She continued through, unable to stop smiling at the mechanical marvels surrounding her.

The next room held exquisite watercolor paintings alongside long silk tapestries hanging from invisible

wires. Some paintings were no more than a single perfect brushstroke that conjured a simple yet breathtaking fish or stalk of bamboo. Clay sculptures in various states of completion lined shelves at the far end of the gallery.

And then, another spiral staircase. Bernadette gasped. Fluffy clouds of pink, violet, and blue hung from the ceiling. She felt as though she was descending from the sky. The stairs ended in the largest hall yet. Here were hundreds of small lighter-than-air balloons, all painted magnificently. Each balloon was anchored to a podium. The walls featured enormous paintings of balloon launches and massive aerial maps of France. At the far end stood a balloon basket the size of a one-story house. Round windows were built into the wicker. As Bernadette approached, the door of the basket opened and a group of men and women stepped out.

"Welcome to the haven of artists and aeronauts, poets and explorers," said one of the women. "Welcome to the Society of Dreamers."

~∂~ Chapter Fourteen ~∂~

Jean-Luc crawled through the window and landed on his bottom. He sighed, stood, and dusted himself off.

Reconnaissance was not the duck's favorite activity. He much preferred analyzing the situation while someone else, preferably Pierre, did the scouting. Alas, there was nothing for it. He must do his bit. Too much was at stake.

He looked around the room and his prodigious powers of deduction began to click away. Wood panels. Tasteful. A small but well-stocked library. Several comfy chairs. It was a reading room. That was a good sign for a secret society. Too often they concentrated on ridiculous costumes, chanting, and arcane (but highly sanitized) rites for the well-to-do members. Probably no slaughtering on altars here, he thought. As a duck, this was reassuring, even though ducks were rarely used as sacrificial animals. Too clever to be caught.

Jean-Luc carefully opened the door and peered into the hall. Deserted, but lit by candlelight. *Recently* lit, he surmised. He was not alone. Jean-Luc waddled quietly down the corridor. At the top of a staircase, he paused. He placed one webbed foot on the stair, which creaked slightly.

"No matter," muttered the duck.

He hopped up onto the railing and slid down, curving

past two floors. At the bottom, he leaped off and landed without a sound. But then he froze on the spot.

An extremely old man sat behind a high podium, staring down at the duck over his half-moon spectacles.

"Um, good evening," said Jean-Luc.

"Monsieur," said the aged gentleman.

"I seem to have—" began Jean-Luc.

"The meeting has already begun," intoned the gentleman. "You may enter, but please do so quietly."

"Of course," said the duck.

The old gentleman returned his attention to the large book on his podium.

Jean-Luc gently pushed open the doors. A long room occupied with men scribbling into large books lay before him. No one looked up as he entered.

Behind him, a man cleared his throat. The duck jumped a bit.

"Hello," said Jean-Luc. "What, uh, are you all working on in here?"

The man smiled, pleased with the question.

"We are recording and cataloguing facts. Our work is devoted to creating an encyclopedia, the most thorough compendium known to . . . uh . . . man."

The gentleman shifted uncomfortably for a moment, then asked: "I do beg your pardon, monsieur, but . . . are you . . . a duck?"

"Yes. You may call me Jean-Luc, if that helps."

"Oh, dear," said the man. "Monsieur Depardieu!" he called across the hall.

"Is there a problem?" asked Jean-Luc.

"Oh, no," said the gentleman. "It is just that you should meet Monsieur Depardieu. He edits the *D* volume, you see."

Monsieur Depardieu joined them.

"Good evening," said the duck.

"Sacré bleu!" blurted Monsieur Depardieu. He raced back to his desk.

"He must update an entry, of course. We are dedicated to the collection of *all* knowledge."

"A noble pursuit," said Jean-Luc.

"A means to an end," said the gentleman. "Allow me to show you the rest of our chambers."

He led Jean-Luc past the desks of scholars and scribes, through a vast library with shelves reaching two stories up with a balcony and ladders on a wheeled track that circled the room.

Jean-Luc paused, admiring the library. He looked across the room. A cat lay on a velvet pillow. They stared at each other for a moment.

"This way, if you please," said the gentleman.

The next room housed maps and charts spread out on

oak tables. Enormous globes sat on pedestals throughout the chamber. Men stood by each of the tables, consulting and arguing quietly. Jean-Luc noticed that each table was labeled with the name of a country, along with the words *Actual* or *Potential Conflict*.

"You see, we believe that knowledge is power,"

continued the gentleman. "Power is sustained through strategy."

Jean-Luc stared at the room of men absorbed in plotting, espionage, subterfuge, and warfare.

"You have entered the Society of Schemers. You are most welcome."

~ Chapter Fifteen ~

$\mathcal{P}$ierre descended a staircase in complete silence. At the foot of the stairs was a corridor, lit by torches. Paintings in elaborate frames lined the walls.

Pierre paused to examine the paintings. Each one featured Cagliostro. Cagliostro with a set of rolled-up plans as the pyramids were being built behind him. Cagliostro cutting a ribbon at the opening of the Parthenon. Cagliostro with Julius Caesar. Cagliostro painting the Sistine Chapel beside Michelangelo.

The rooster continued down the corridor. He paused to listen at a door, then pushed it open. Beyond was a high-ceilinged chamber, like a church. Pews lined the sides, leading to a platform and altar.

Cagliostro himself, cloaked and wearing his strange, birdlike mask, stood by the altar. Mozart, Guillotin, and Lavoisier sat in the pews. Franz Mesmer and Bancroft stood at the foot of the platform below Cagliostro.

"Welcome, Bête Noire," intoned Cagliostro, "to the Society of Rogues."

"Charming," said Pierre. "These secret societies are so quaint. Why the mask, Cagliostro? Judging from the artwork, I would say that everyone knows who you are."

Cagliostro chuckled in his deep baritone voice. "'Why the mask?' asks the rooster in a black satin mask."

"Without my mask, I can blend in with any ordinary rooster," said Pierre.

"Oh, I doubt that very much indeed," rumbled Cagliostro.

"Well, be that as it may," continued Pierre, "I did hope to have a look around without your knowledge."

"I know all," said Cagliostro. "I have lived for millennia—"

"You are the King of Liars. A charlatan. A fraud. A fake," said Pierre.

"Please do go on," said Cagliostro.

"I think that covers it. Where is Benjamin Franklin?"

"Around here somewhere. He enjoys our sparkling company."

"And your mayonnaise?" asked Pierre.

At the mention of the word *mayonnaise*, the observers in the pews stood and drew swords.

"Tsk, tsk. Now look what you have done," said Cagliostro.

Mesmer snapped his fingers and they all filed out and stood in a line before the altar.

"Perhaps you know a bit too much . . . for a rooster," said Cagliostro.

Pierre drew his sword. "I have been told that on occasion."

The line of noble captives attacked. Pierre defended himself but did not strike back. These people were, after all, under Mesmer's power of suggestion. As they advanced, he had no choice but to retreat. The attackers thrust their swords in unison, and Pierre fell backward through a heavy velvet curtain.

He tumbled down a steep stone staircase and came to a stop in a large, round, dark chamber. Benjamin Franklin stood motionless in the center of the room. Two additional heavy doors were set in the chamber walls. Pierre's sword laid at the foot of the stairs.

The mesmerized mob entered, followed by Cagliostro, Mesmer, and Bancroft.

"I see we are the first to arrive," said Cagliostro. He clapped his hands, and torches ignited throughout the chamber.

"I do like that trick," said Pierre.

"Perhaps I will teach it to you," said Cagliostro, picking up Pierre's sword and tossing it aside. "Ah, here they come now."

The two doors opened. Bernadette and the Dreamers entered from one, Jean-Luc and the Schemers from the other.

"Turns out Cagliostro was in my secret society," Pierre called to the others.

"I am not so sure there were ever three choices," said Jean-Luc.

Bernadette saw Franklin and turned to Cagliostro.

"Where is the notebook?"

"Gone," said Cagliostro. "Or more precisely, sold. King Louis offered a great sum for 'my' inventions. He plans to set up the Heat Ray along the Channel and use it on the British navy. I may have suggested that, actually."

"No," said Bernadette.

"Oh, assuredly," said Cagliostro. "The idea came from the most strategic minds in the land." Cagliostro indicated the Society of Schemers, who bowed.

"But why start a war?" asked Pierre. "What do you get from that?"

"Nothing," said Cagliostro. "Directly. *Indirectly* I will benefit from France and England being occupied with their own mutual destruction. That will allow me to fly to the newly minted United States, courtesy of the most extraordinary balloons created by the Society of Dreamers."

Cagliostro clapped politely at the Society of Dreamers, who also bowed.

"And then, with the endorsement of my very good friend Benjamin Franklin, I shall become the *King of America*."

Franklin didn't so much as blink. Mesmer waved his wand at him for good measure.

"That is absurd," said Bernadette.

"Perhaps not. A few promises here, a claim of enormous wealth and power there. The New World should be fairly susceptible to . . . what did you call me, Pierre? A charlatan. The King of Liars."

Cagliostro strode across the chamber to a tall black curtain.

"I have impressed even myself. Yet this plan could not be designed and executed by me alone. I needed a team. A team inspired by whispers . . . rumors . . . legends."

Cagliostro pulled a rope and the curtain parted,

exposing a banner with the words:

THE SOCIETY

OF

SCHEMERS

ROGUES

DREAMERS

He waved his hand and some of the letters vanished, leaving:

THE SOCIETY

OF

S

R

D

He waved once more and the banner now read:

ＴＨＥ ＳＯＣＩＥＴＹ

ＯＦ

ＳＨＥＥＰ

ＲＯＯＳＴＥＲ

ＤＵＣＫ

"Three societies banded together," said Cagliostro. "All I needed to provide . . . was you."

A cage lowered from the ceiling. Cagliostro's highwaymen appeared from the shadows. They seized Bernadette, Jean-Luc, and Pierre, shoved them into the cage, and locked the door. The cage rose once again into the air and dangled in front of the banner.

"A prize none could resist," said Cagliostro.

Chapter Sixteen

At the secret headquarters in Trianon, Emile picked up a wooden cup from the worktable.

"Put that down," said Sophie.

"But it's empty," said Emile.

"Put it back *exactly* where it was," said Sophie.

"It'll leave a little ring," said Emile.

Sophie glared. Emile put the cup down in the exact same spot.

He sighed. He shifted on his stool. They had been

waiting a long time. Sophie mostly ignored him. But now she paced the room, grumbling.

"I cannot stand this," said Sophie.

"We were told to wait."

"Do you always do as you are told?"

"Yes," said Emile. "Whenever possible."

"Well, this is *im*possible," growled Sophie. She kicked over a stool.

Emile started to rise.

"I swear, if you pick that up . . . "

"Sorry," said Emile, sitting again.

Finally Sophie stopped pacing. She lifted the stool and plunked down across from Emile.

"No, I'm sorry," she said quietly. "You are right. Bernadette, Jean-Luc, and Pierre said to wait. That's what we need to do."

"You really admire them," said Emile.

"They are extraordinary," said Sophie. "They saved my life."

"How?" asked Emile.

"Inspiration," said Sophie. "I was simply the daughter

of a good but poor peasant," she went on. "I thought life
was very limited."

Sophie gestured toward the designs on the walls, the
shelves of inventions, the maps of the world.

"Then I met Bernadette. She *saw* something in me, something I didn't even see in myself. She trusted me. When she showed me her balloon designs . . . well . . . that was it. I never knew such wonders could exist."

Emile listened without a word. Sophie continued.

"I flew my first balloon when I was nine years old. Bernadette showed me how. And not just little things a small girl could do. She taught me how to properly fly. And now I am an aeronaut. One day I will fly around the entire world in a balloon. Just watch."

"I believe you," said Emile.

Sophie studied him for a moment.

"Thank you," she said quietly.

"For what?"

"Believing."

Sophie stood and crossed the room to the wall of

balloon designs. Emile could no longer see her face. He thought that might have been intentional.

"You did well," said Sophie, her back still to Emile. "In the balloon. You did not panic or get in the way. I was glad you were there."

"Only a few days ago, I was content with my routine," said Emile. "My position as caretaker was all the challenge I thought I needed. But now . . . the last two days have been terrifying and worrisome and horribly chaotic, and part of me would love to just straighten up a bit in here. Yet, for the first time, I feel like I might be capable of more than just caretaking. Perhaps I have some potential of my own."

Sophie turned and smiled at Emile.

"But, since we're waiting, maybe I *could* just straighten some of these—"

"Touch anything and I will clobber you."

A bone-chilling sound came from above. Part scream, part meow.

Sophie and Emile carefully opened the trapdoor and peered into the dark barn.

"I thought that might get your attention," said the cat. "I have a message from the duck. They need you."

Chapter Seventeen

The cage twisted slowly above the society members. All eyes were on the sheep, rooster, and duck.

A messenger arrived and handed Cagliostro a letter.

"My, my," said Cagliostro. "It seems my presence is requested at the palace. They have prepared a prototype of my Heat Ray."

"So soon?" asked Mesmer.

"Yes. The genius of the design relies on extensive use of mirrors. And if Versailles has anything, it's mirrors."

Cagliostro waved to the cage. "You must excuse me, but I am sure the society will keep you comfortable and entertained. They have much to ask. Mesmer, Bancroft, please gather Monsieur Franklin and his cohorts and follow me. I think we shall all enjoy this demonstration. Adieu!"

The door closed. The cage turned slightly, suspended above the remaining society members, who stared up in awe.

Bernadette, Jean-Luc, and Pierre remained silent.

Someone cleared his throat nervously.

"We, um, are sorry about the cage. Necessary but unpleasant," said one of the members.

"Yes, we do hope of course that you will come to enjoy living here in the society. At which point, we would be glad to release you from the cage," said another.

"Or perhaps move you to a larger cage on the ground," another hastened to add.

The cage twisted slowly, the chain creaking.

"Please speak to us, oh Sheep, Rooster, and Duck!" cried one society member. "We have much to learn from you!"

Silence.

"Yes, please," said an aeronaut. "Why not make the most of this time together?"

"We *are* making the most of our time," said Bernadette.

The society members exchanged perplexed looks.

"We are escaping," said Pierre with a yawn.

The cage turned slowly. No one moved.

"How?" someone finally asked.

"Three key ingredients," said Jean-Luc.

Number one . . . friends.

This way, if you please.

I had not seen the cat for two years.

But we both remembered our last meeting.

You can count on me.

And how about you? What have you learned tonight?

Height is not a barrier to success.

Neither is species. I am sure you will go far, Napoleon.

WINK

Number two . . .
imagination.

And number
three . . .

. . . daring!

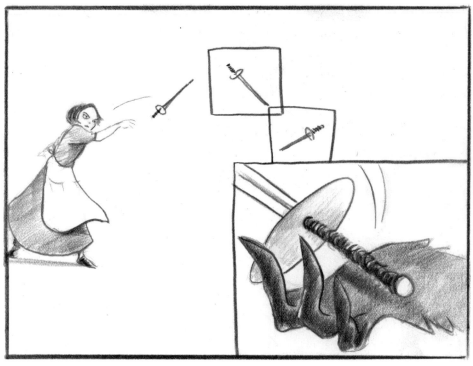

Chapter Eighteen

The Heat Ray device had been constructed on a hill behind the Palace of Versailles. A crowd of nobility was in attendance, including King Louis XVI and Queen Marie Antoinette. Cagliostro bowed to the king. Franklin, Mesmer, Bancroft, Guillotin, and Lavoisier followed suit. Mesmer held his wand behind Franklin's back.

"Your Majesty," said Cagliostro, "I commend you on your speedy assembly of my device."

"I like to make sure major investments *function*, Cagliostro, before paying in full."

"No need to worry. My design is quite ingenious. The Heat Ray will certainly work to your satisfaction."

The king smirked. "And to the British navy's *dis*satisfaction once the weapon is in place along the Channel."

"Yes," said Cagliostro. "As formidable as sailing vessels are, they are still quite flammable."

"Good to see you, too, Franklin," said the king. "You know, I am surprised that *you* did not think of such a marvelous machine."

Franklin stared at the Heat Ray. He twitched. Mesmer pressed his wand against Franklin's back.

"Mayonnaise," murmured Mesmer.

"Never touch the stuff," said the king. "Shall we begin?"

"Your Majesty," said a courtier. "We need a target of some kind."

"Ah, yes," said the king. "Good point."

"Might I suggest," said Cagliostro with a charming smile, "the barn in yonder Trianon?"

"My barn!" exclaimed Marie Antoinette. "Are you mad?"

Cagliostro swept to Marie Antoinette, took her hand, and bowed low.

"I have been called mad before, but not for many centuries," purred Cagliostro.

"Oh, Cagliostro," said Marie Antoinette, lightly tapping his shoulder with her fan.

"I merely suggest the barn because . . . Oh, I had wanted to keep this a *secret* . . . for your birthday."

"My birthday? A present? Do tell."

"It will spoil the surprise."

"I command you, you saucy sorcerer," said Marie Antoinette.

"Ah," said Cagliostro. "If I must. I had planned to build you a new barn based on the one I built for Alexander the Great in three twenty-seven BC."

"Alexander the Great!"

"He kept elephants in his."

"I want it!"

"You shall have it, my Queen."

"Burn the barn!" said Marie Antoinette. "Oh, but wait. What of the animals?"

"Your Majesty," said Cagliostro, "you can always get another sheep, rooster, and duck."

Franklin gazed down the hill toward the pretend village of Trianon. He stared at the barn. Something stirred in his clouded mind. The barnyard. A sheep. A rooster. A duck.

"Begin the demonstration," commanded the king.

Levers were pulled, gears turned, the row of reflecting

mirrors angled up to catch the rays of the sun.

Franklin rubbed his eyes.

Sheep.

Rooster.

Duck.

Beams of concentrated light shot from the mirrors into an enormous brass box that had a large musket-like muzzle sticking out of the front. The box began to shake. Vials of various colored liquids boiled along the sides of the box. A fan whirred. A loud hum filled the air.

Franklin closed his eyes.

And he remembered.

He was aloft in a balloon. There was great excitement. Emile was there and a girl named Sophie. And . . . a sheep, a rooster, and a duck. The animals were protecting him. They were in charge and fighting for their lives.

"Stop!" yelled Franklin.

The muzzle of the Heat Ray was aimed at the barn.

"Now!" shouted Cagliostro.

A soldier pulled a red lever on the side of the weapon.

Bubbles poured out of the machine. Big and small,

pink and blue, the bubbles trickled out of the Heat Ray and floated up into the sky.

"What is the meaning of this?" demanded the king.

Cagliostro, for the first time in many years, was at a loss for words.

Everyone watched as the bubbles floated up to the clouds. And then, from above the clouds, a sleek and magnificent balloon descended.

"Oh, how lovely," said Bernadette as they drifted down through the rising bubbles.

The balloon landed and deflated. Emile, Sophie, Bernadette, Jean-Luc, and Pierre burst from the basket.

"Cagliostro!" roared the king. "Explain!"

"Allow me," said Franklin, shoving Mesmer aside and addressing the king. "The Heat Ray is of my design, much to my shame. The plans were stolen by Cagliostro and sold to you."

"I do not care who invented it! Why does it not work?"
The king held out the plans.

Franklin turned to Cagliostro. Cagliostro shrugged.
"I gave them *your* designs, Franklin."

"Then . . . I must admit I am also confused," said Franklin.

"It was not *exactly* your design, Monsieur Franklin."

All turned to Emile. He cleared his throat.

"I drew in your notebook, Monsieur Franklin. I changed the design before bringing it to you in the carriage."

"You little sneak," hissed Bancroft.

Franklin took the notebook from the king and examined the altered plans.

"A perfect forgery. Very artfully done," said Franklin. He looked at Emile. Emile gulped. Then Franklin smiled. "Excellent initiative, my good lad."

"Thank you, Monsieur."

"Yes, good work, Emile," said Jean-Luc. He waddled

up to the king. "But Cagliostro's plot was far from innocent, Your Majesty."

The king, queen, and gathered nobility all stared down at the talking duck.

Bernadette joined Jean-Luc. "His plan was to incite a war with England and to use the distraction to conquer America," said the sheep. "He was going to invade with balloons—a completely vulgar use of the invention."

"The King of Liars," said Pierre, "is a menace to all creatures."

Silence.

"I am sorry," said King Louis. "But . . . " He looked up. "Talking animals?"

Montgolfier strode from the assembled nobility.

"May I introduce Your Majesties to Bernadette, Pierre, and Jean-Luc. They have been protecting France for a very long time."

"Oh," said the king, turning back to the animals. "*Merci.*"

"Don't mention it," said Jean-Luc.

Cagliostro turned to Mesmer and Bancroft. "I think we should bid adieu."

They started to run, but the path was instantly blocked by a masked rooster with a sword.

"Bête Noire," growled Cagliostro.

"At your service," said Pierre. And with a swipe of his blade, he knocked Mesmer's wand out of his hand.

The king's guards surrounded the men.

Cagliostro laughed.

"Well, *c'est la vie!*" he said brightly. He turned to Bernadette, Jean-Luc, and Pierre. "I do look forward to our next meeting."

"They do not allow visitors in the Bastille," said Jean-Luc.

"The Bastille?" chuckled Cagliostro. "I certainly do not want to be *there* for long."

The guards marched the sorcerer, hypnotist, and spy away.

~ Chapter Nineteen ~

*O*nce the royalty and charlatans had gone, Sophie, Emile, Franklin, and Montgolfier strolled the grounds of

Versailles with Bernadette, Jean-Luc, and Pierre.

"That takes care of Cagliostro, for now anyway," said Jean-Luc. "But I fear we may need a new headquarters."

"Yes," said Bernadette. "I cannot imagine working on new balloon designs with Marie Antoinette looking over my shoulder."

"She'll want all the balloons to be pink and sparkly," said Sophie. "Pfft."

"You know," said Benjamin Franklin. "My time here

in France is ending. I must return to my scrappy-yet-fragile fledgling nation. There is much to do to ensure a strong, honest democracy."

"You shall be missed by all of France," said Montgolfier.

"And I shall miss you," said Franklin. "It might be nice to keep my home in Passy, in case of a return visit. However, I would hate for it to sit empty."

He stopped and addressed Bernadette.

"Perhaps you three might find my château suitable for your endeavors? There is room for all, a fine library, and a barn that would make an excellent workshop," said Franklin. "Sophie, you and your father are welcome as well."

Franklin put his hand on Emile's shoulder. "And, of course, my dear, loyal Emile. You must call it home."

"I will take care of it, Monsieur Franklin," said Emile.

"You know, Emile," said Montgolfier. "In addition to balloon work, my brother and I own the finest paper company in France. We supply *all* of the great artists. Perhaps you would like to work for me? We could use your artistic eye and initiative."

"That sounds wonderful," said Emile.

"Free drawing paper as a perk, I would expect?" asked Franklin.

"But of course," said Montgolfier.

"I could still clean around the house," Emile whispered to the others.

"If that brings you joy," said Bernadette.

"It does, actually," said Emile.

"We will work on that," said Pierre.

"That's settled, then," said Franklin.

The group walked along quietly. Night had fallen, and the moon was full and bright.

"I wonder, Bernadette, Jean-Luc, and Pierre. What is next for you?" asked Franklin.

They stopped and gazed up at the moon.

Franklin smiled.

Emile looked at the moon, then at Sophie. "Surely not?"

"Why not?" Sophie laughed.

"I am not saying it would be impossible," said Jean-Luc. "But it might take some time."

"How much time?" asked Montgolfier.

Bernadette's eyes filled with the reflection of the moon. She turned to her friends. Pierre nodded. Jean-Luc shrugged.

"June," said the sheep, the rooster, and the duck.

~ Author's Note ~

$\mathcal{I}$t is said that truth is stranger than fiction. In the case of France in the 1780s, the truth may not be as strange as the particular fiction in *The Sheep, the Rooster, and the Duck*, but it's close. Charlatans, spies, and secret societies were everywhere. Science and mysticism were battling it out. And everyone was captivated by the wonder of the lighter-than-air balloon.

So what is true? Which characters really lived?

Benjamin Franklin was in France at this time lobbying for help in the American Revolution. Franklin invented many things in his extraordinary life (including the glass armonica that Mozart—also a real historical figure—plays in the story). If anyone could have invented a heat ray, it would have been him. There were rumors about this at the time, but no proof—in a journal or otherwise—was ever found.

Franklin did employ a secretary named Edward Bancroft, who was, indeed, an English spy. Bancroft truly did send reports in the form of love letters, with the real information written in invisible ink between the lines.

Count Cagliostro, aka Joseph Balsamo, was an Italian forger, magician, charmer, and all-around scoundrel who frequented European courts. Author Alexandre Dumas was so fascinated by Cagliostro that he made him the villain in several books. Cagliostro has been a character in operas, novels, comic books, and movies since the nineteenth century. It seems that his claim of immortality might be true after all.

Franz Anton Mesmer believed that a natural force—animal magnetism—existed in all living and inanimate objects. He claimed that he could cure various conditions by manipulating these forces. This became known as mesmerism. Benjamin Franklin and his team (including the future inventor of the guillotine) investigated Mesmer by request of the king. They concluded that mesmerism only worked if the subject believed that it would work. Today, this is known as the placebo effect. Mesmer, disgraced, was sent into exile.

Queen Marie Antoinette did have a pretend village where she could "dress casual" and contemplate the simple life of a French peasant. Unfortunately, she did not contemplate too deeply. This would cost her more than her toy village when the French people eventually revolted and overthrew the monarchy.

Joseph-Michel Montgolfier and his brother Jacques-Étienne owned a paper-manufacturing business and were fascinated with building lighter-than-air balloons. Their paper business, renamed Canson in the early 1800s, still exists today. I use Canson sketchbooks for my illustrations.

The famous flight of the Montgolfier balloon—the first with living pilots—occurred at Versailles on September 19, 1783. I learned about the event from an exhibit at the Museum of the American Philosophical Society in Philadelphia. I was captivated by a small drawing of the flight, and it sparked an idea that became this story many years later.

The sheep, the rooster, and the duck were real. They did pilot that balloon in 1783. But what, you may ask, did they do *after* the flight?

Well . . . no one knows for sure.

For Nora and Jasper, with special thanks

to David Niven, Tyrone Power, and Orson Welles

The Sheep, the Rooster, and the Duck
Text and illustrations copyright © 2022 by Matt Phelan

www.harpercollinschildrens.com

The text of this book is set in Fournier MT.
Book design by Sylvie Le Floc'h

Library of Congress Cataloging-in-Publication Data is available.
ISBN 978-0-06-291100-1 (hardcover)
22 23 24 25 26 PC/LSCH 10 9 8 7 6 5 4 3 2 1
First Edition
Greenwillow Books